First BEDTIME STORIES

Jenny Wood

Illustrated by Carol Lawson

GALLERY BOOKS

An Imprint of W. H. Smith Publishers Inc.

112 Madison Avenue

New York City 10016

THIS BOOK BELONGS TO

Project editor: Jane O'Shea
Editor: Sue Hook
Art editor: Paul Welti

First published in 1990 by
Conran Octopus Limited
37 Shelton Street, London WC2H 9HN

© *text 1990 Conran Octopus Limited*
© *illustration 1990 Carol Lawson*

First published in the United States in 1991 by Gallery Books,
an imprint of W.H. Smith Publishers, Inc.,
112 Madison Avenue, New York, New York 10016

Gallery Books are available for bulk purchase for sales
promotions and premium use. For details write or telephone
the Manager of Special Sales, W.H. Smith Publishers, Inc.,
112 Madison Avenue, New York, New York 10016. (212) 532-6600

ISBN 0-8317-3360-8

CONTENTS

THE FOOLISH RABBIT

I N THE JUNGLE, LONG AGO, A RABBIT LAY asleep. He was dreaming, and in his dream the world was falling to pieces. Suddenly a monkey dropped a coconut from a tree. It thudded on to the ground behind the sleeping rabbit. The rabbit was woken by the noise, and jumped to his feet at once. 'Oh, no!' he cried. 'I wasn't dreaming after all! The world *is* falling to pieces!' And off he ran, as fast as his legs would carry him.

He ran past another rabbit who called out, 'Why are you running so fast?'

'Haven't you heard?' said the first rabbit. 'The world is falling to pieces!'

The second rabbit began to run too. The two rabbits met another rabbit, and another, until soon there were hundreds of rabbits running as fast as they could.

The rabbits met a deer and she joined in too. Then the deer saw a fox, and the fox saw an elephant. Together, all the animals raced through the jungle.

Soon they passed the lion. He heard them cry out that the world was falling to pieces, but he didn't believe them. He roared loudly.

All the animals stopped as soon as they heard the lion's roar, for the lion, after all, is King of the Jungle.

'Why are you all running so fast?' asked the lion.

'Because the world is falling to pieces!' they chorused.

'How do you know?' said the lion.

'The fox told me,' replied the elephant.

'The deer told me,' added the fox.

'One of the rabbits told me,' whispered the deer.

'Which rabbit?' bellowed the lion.

The little rabbit stepped forward.

'How do you know that the world is falling to pieces?' asked the lion.

'I heard it,' gasped the rabbit.

'Show me where you heard it,' said the lion.

So all the animals ran back to where the rabbit had been sleeping. There, on the ground, lay the coconut. The lion looked at it.

'This coconut must have fallen out of the tree while you were asleep!' he laughed. 'That's the noise you heard, you silly rabbit.'

The animals heaved a huge sigh of relief. The world was not falling apart after all.

'Thank you,' they said to the lion. 'You are so very wise. We might have continued running for ever.'

THE SUN AND THE WIND

THE WIND HAD BEEN BLOWING VERY HARD ALL morning. By lunchtime he was really beginning to feel very pleased with himself. He looked at the sun who was beaming brightly above the hilltops.

'I'm stronger than you,' said the wind to the sun.

'No, you're not,' the sun smiled back.

'Yes, I am,' repeated the wind.

'No, you're not,' insisted the sun.

'Yes, I am.'

'No, you're not.' The sun began to get rather angry.

'Very well then,' said the wind. 'Do you see that man down there? Let's see which of us can be the first to make him take off his coat.'

'Alright,' said the sun. 'I agree.'

So the wind began to blow. He puffed and puffed for all he was worth and the man's coat flapped in the strong breeze. But the more the wind blew, the more the man hugged his coat closely to him. He would *not* take it off.

'Now it's my turn,' smiled the sun.

The sun shone his sunny beams all over the man's face and body. The man began to feel warmer and warmer. He unbuttoned his coat. The sun's rays beat down until the man felt so hot he took off his coat and sat down.

'I've won,' laughed the sun.

THE MARK OF
AN ANGEL

ONCE UPON A TIME A LITTLE GIRL FELL ASLEEP in the long grass at the bottom of her garden. She had been playing in the sunshine all day long, and was soon fast asleep.

As she lay there, she was seen by an angel.

'What a pretty child!' whispered the angel to herself. 'She must have been stolen from Heaven.'

So the angel flew down to the garden, and touched the little girl's cheeks just at the places where a smile ends.

As soon as she touched her, she realised that this was a human child who belonged on the earth, not in Heaven. So leaving the little girl to sleep peacefully, she flew away.

But the angel's fingers had left soft marks on the little girl's skin. That is why, when she smiles now, two little dimples appear, one on each cheek.

THE LITTLE BLUE ENGINE

T HE LITTLE TRAIN PUFFED ALONG MERRILY. Her cars were full of toys and food for the children on the other side of the mountain. There were teddy bears, cars, airplanes, dolls, books and every other kind of toy you could ever wish for. And there were rosy apples, juicy oranges, lollipops and nuts. 'Toot, toot!' said the little train proudly.

Then, all of a sudden, she stopped. 'Oh, dear!' cried all the toys. 'What's the matter?'

The little train looked sad. She didn't know why, but she seemed to be stuck. Her wheels just wouldn't move.

'Don't worry,' said the toy clown. 'Here comes a shiny new engine. We'll ask him to help us.'

But the shiny new engine just snorted. 'I'm much too new and important to pull you over the mountain!' he said. And off he went.

The toys looked sad. It seemed as if the children wouldn't get their presents after all. But the clown was sure everything would work out allright in the end.

'Look!' he cried. 'Here's another engine. He looks very big and strong. Let's ask him if he will help us.'

But the big strong engine just laughed. 'I'm far too big and strong to pull such a tiny little train,' he boomed. 'I pull trains which are loaded with big machines for factories. I couldn't possibly pull a trainload of toys!' And off he went.

But the toy clown didn't give up. In the distance he could see a little blue engine. It was a very tiny engine, but it seemed friendly and cheerful.

'Little blue engine,' shouted all the toys. 'Can you please help us take all these gifts to the children on the other side of the mountain?'

'Well, I'm very tiny,' said the little blue engine, 'but I'll try!' And she hitched herself to the little train.

'Hurray!' shouted the toys as the little blue engine tugged and pulled and tugged and pulled. Slowly, the train began to move again.

Up and up climbed the little blue engine until at last she reached the top of the mountain. Then down, down she went to the town in the valley where the girls and boys lived. The toys all cheered, and the little blue engine puffed proudly.

'I knew I could,' she said.

THE FAIRY MOUND

O NE BRIGHT SUMMER'S DAY, A WOMAN WAS IN her kitchen baking bread. Her baby daughter was playing on a rug nearby.

Suddenly, the back door opened. The woman looked around and saw a beautiful lady standing there. She looked as though she was very tired.

'Come in,' said the woman. 'Come in and sit down.'

'You're very kind,' said the lady, 'but I am in a hurry. I have come to ask if you will do something for me.'

Just at that moment, the baby put out her hand to grasp the lady's fine green gown. But her hand closed on nothing, as if she had tried to grasp a sunbeam. Startled, the woman realized that the lady was a fairy!

'If it is something I can do, then I will be happy to do it,' the woman replied, stumbling over her words a little because she had never in her life come face to face with a fairy before.

'Every time you throw your dish water on to the green mound near your back door,' explained the fairy, 'the water soaks through the grass and drips down on to my bed below.'

'Oh, I'm so sorry,' exclaimed the woman. 'I had no idea! I promise I will never again throw water on to the green mound.'

'Thank you,' smiled the fairy. 'And as you've been so kind, I would now like to help you. If you ever find you do not have time to mend your children's clothes or make new clothes for them, just leave your things on the green mound before you go to bed.'

And with that, the fairy slipped silently away.

After the fairy's visit, the woman often left wool and linen on the green mound. The following morning she found jerseys knitted and clothes sewn and ready to wear. For the fairies, you see, sleep all day and work all through the night.

Never again was any water thrown on the green mound. And on still, silent nights the woman often heard the fairies singing sweetly as they went peacefully about their work.

WHY THE BEAR
HAS A STUMPY TAIL

ONE DAY, IN THE MIDDLE OF WINTER, THE FOX came slinking home with a string of fish he had stolen from a poor, unfortunate fisherman. On the way, he met the bear.

'Where did you get all those fish?' gasped the bear, licking his lips at the sight of so much delicious food.

'I caught them myself,' replied the fox proudly.

'Goodness me!' exclaimed the bear. 'You must be very clever. Will you teach me how to catch fish too?'

'Oh, it's terribly easy,' smiled the sly fox. 'All you have to do is cut a hole in the ice and put your tail down into it. You must sit there for as long as possible. Don't worry if your tail starts to sting a little – that means that the fish are biting. The longer you stay, the more fish you will catch. Then, when you are ready, give a strong sideways pull and your tail and all the fish will come free!'

The bear did exactly as the fox told him. He held his tail in the ice for a long, long time, dreaming of all the fish he would be able to eat for supper. But when he gave a strong sideways pull, his tail snapped right off! It had frozen in the icy water. And that is why the bear goes about with only a stump of a tail to this very day.

THE OSTRICH AND THE HEDGEHOG

ONCE UPON A TIME, THE OSTRICH AND THE hedgehog had a quarrel about which of them could run faster.

'Me, of course,' boasted the ostrich.

'Will you race against me?' asked the hedgehog.

'Of course I will,' laughed the ostrich. 'But you have absolutely no chance of winning!'

'We'll see,' said the hedgehog quietly.

The next day, the ostrich and the hedgehog met at the barley field. 'One, two, three,' the ostrich counted, and as he said 'three', the race began.

The ostrich seemed to fly down the field with his giant strides. But just as he neared the end, up popped the hedgehog ahead of him. The ostrich couldn't believe it.

'Impossible!' he screeched angrily.

But there was no doubt that the hedgehog had won.

What the ostrich didn't realize, of course, was that one hedgehog looks much like another. While the first hedgehog began the race at one end of the field, his friend hid at the other end and popped up as soon as the ostrich approached.

POOR ZIPPY

ONE MORNING RITA THE HEN HEARD A MOST peculiar noise. She looked around. Poor Zippy, one of her chicks, had pecked at a bean which had got stuck in his throat. At once, Rita ran to the cow.

'Oh, cow,' she pleaded, 'please give me some butter. My poor little chick, Zippy, has a bean stuck in his throat.'

'I'd be delighted to give you some butter for Zippy,' said the cow. 'But first, I'd like you to get me some hay from the haymakers.'

Rita ran to the haymakers. 'Please give me some hay for the cow,' she begged. 'If you do, then the cow will give me some butter for my poor little chick, Zippy, who has a bean stuck in his throat.'

'Of course we will,' said the haymakers. 'But first, we'd like you to get us some buns from the baker.'

Rita ran to the baker's shop. 'Mr Baker,' she gasped, for by now she was a little out of breath, 'please give me some buns for the haymakers. If you do, they will give me hay for the cow, who will give me butter for my poor little chick, Zippy, who has a bean stuck in his throat.'

'I'll be glad to,' said the baker. 'But first, I'd like you to bring me some firewood from the woodcutter.'

'Please give me some firewood for the baker,' panted Rita when she found the woodcutter. 'If you do, then he will give me buns for the haymakers, who will give me hay for the cow, who will give me butter for my poor little chick, Zippy, who has a bean stuck in his throat.'

'I will give you some firewood,' said the woodcutter. 'But I'll need an axe from the blacksmith. I've lost mine.'

So off ran Rita again. 'Please give me an axe for the woodcutter,' she cried when she saw the blacksmith. 'If you do, he'll give me firewood for the baker, who will give me buns for the haymakers, who will give me hay for the cow, who will give me butter for my poor little chick, Zippy, who has a bean stuck in his throat.'

But the blacksmith needed iron to make the axe, so Rita had to run to the little people who lived under the mountain and looked after all the iron inside the earth. They carried a huge pile of iron to the blacksmith.

At once the blacksmith made an axe. The woodcutter used it to chop firewood. The baker lit a fire with the firewood and baked some delicious buns. Rita carried these to the haymakers who gave her some hay. And finally, the cow gave her some butter. Rita ran quickly to her poor little chick, Zippy, who swallowed the butter and the bean with it! Soon he was happily pecking about in the farmyard once again.

THE KNIGHT'S TEN THOUSAND JEWELS

A KNIGHT WAS ONCE WALKING ALONG THE seashore when he saw a hideous monster rise from the waves and creep on to the sand. The knight drew his sword at once. 'Who are you?' he cried.

'My name is Dragonstar,' the creature replied. 'The Dragon King of the sea is angry with me and has forbidden me to stay in my home beneath the waves. You can kill me if you like. Even if you do not, I shall soon die, because I cannot live long on land.'

The knight felt sorry for the monster, and took it home. He let it live in a lake fringed with graceful trees.

All went well until the knight fell in love with a beautiful lady who refused to marry him unless he gave her ten thousand jewels. The knight knew that he could not afford such an expensive present. But he loved her very much, and he grew sad.

Dragonstar did not know the reason for his master's unhappiness, but he hated to see him so miserable. One day he just burst into tears. The knight stared at him in amazement. Every tear that fell from the creature's eyes was a precious jewel!

'You have saved me, Dragonstar!' he cried. Then his face fell, for he realized that there were not yet ten thousand jewels.

'Please weep again,' he begged.

Dragonstar was annoyed. 'I cannot cry whenever you want me to!' he snapped.

But when the knight told his story, Dragonstar said at once, 'Take me back to the sea and let me look at my old home. Perhaps then I will be able to cry again.'

So the knight and the monster travelled to the shore. Soon large tears began to fall from Dragonstar's eyes. Once again, each tear was a precious jewel. The pile of jewels grew and grew, until there were more than enough for the knight to win his bride.

Just then, a voice came from the sea.

'You are pardoned, Dragonstar. You may return to your home.'

Dragonstar was overjoyed. He and the knight said goodbye and parted, one for his bride, the other for his beloved sea.

THE DINKEY-DANKEY DONKEY

T HERE WAS ONCE A MAN WHO HAD NOTHING in the world but the clothes he wore, and a donkey. The donkey was a skinny old thing, but it was all the man could sell to get money for food. He knew that he couldn't sell it in his own country, where people would take one look at it and refuse to pay good money for anything so old and bony. So off he went to find a country where the people had never seen a donkey.

After a while, he came to a land where the people looked at the donkey in amazement. 'It's a dinkey,' said one. 'No, no, it's a dankey,' said another.

Soon the king got to hear of this dinkey-dankey, and he ordered the poor man to bring the animal to the palace.

'I will buy this dinkey-dankey,' said the king. 'How much will it cost?'

'It's not a dinkey-dankey,' explained the man. 'It's a donkey. And I'll sell it for two hundred gold coins.'

The king agreed at once. The poor man couldn't believe his luck. He took his bag of gold and went home.

As for the donkey, he was given as much food as he could eat. But the people of that country still call him a dinkey-dankey to this very day.

THE LION AND THE MOUSE

ONCE, WHEN A LION WAS ASLEEP, A LITTLE mouse began running up and down on his back. The mouse's tiny feet ruffled the lion's fur and tickled his skin. The lion soon woke up, very angry at being disturbed. He grabbed the little mouse in his enormous paw and, giving a great roar, opened his huge jaws ready to swallow the tiny creature in one gulp.

'Oh, please, King Lion, don't eat me!' squeaked the mouse. 'I didn't mean any harm. If you will only let me go, I will never ever forget your kindness. And perhaps I'll be able to do something to help you one day.'

The lion found the idea of a tiny mouse being able to help him, the King of the Jungle, so funny that he lifted his paw and let the mouse go.

A few days later, the mouse heard the lion roaring angrily and went to find out what had happened. He found the lion caught in a hunter's net. Remembering his promise, the little mouse set to work nibbling at the net with his sharp teeth. Soon, the lion was free.

So the little mouse had been able to do something to help the lion after all. A friend is a friend, no matter how big or small!

THE FAT PANCAKE

THERE WAS ONCE AN OLD WOMAN WHO LIVED in Norway. She had seven hungry children, who liked nothing better than to eat pancakes. One day she decided that, instead of making seven small pancakes, she would cook one enormous pancake for the whole family.

She whisked and stirred the creamy batter in her largest bowl, and soon the pancake was sizzling and browning in her largest frying pan. The children jostled and pushed and jumped up and down. 'What a beautiful, fat pancake!' they cried excitedly.

'Well,' thought the pancake to itself, 'if I'm so beautiful, I'm much too good to be eaten!' And all of a sudden it jumped straight out of the frying pan and out of the door. On it hopped, down the road, with the seven children chasing after it.

But the fat pancake was too fast for the children. It was even too fast for the farm dog who joined in the chase, and too fast for the children's pet goat. It ran away from a farmyard hen who wanted to peck it, and from a cow who wanted to lick it. It ran past the farmer's horse and out over the fields. It was just beginning to feel in need of a rest when it came to a river.

Pancakes cannot swim, so the fat pancake had to think how to get across. Just then, a little pig came up.

'Would you like a lift across the river?' asked the pig.

'Oh, yes, please,' replied the fat pancake.

But no sooner had the pancake jumped on the little pig's back than SNAP! the little pig had bitten the pancake in half and swallowed it.

The other half of the pancake leapt to the ground and raced away, hippity-hop. The little pig tried to catch it, but he was too slow. Soon the pancake was out of sight, over the hills and far away.

And that is why, even today, pigs spend most of their time sniffing the ground. They are still looking for the other half of that deliciously fat, juicy pancake!

THE WHISPERING REEDS

L ONG, LONG AGO, THE GODS OF ANCIENT
Greece held a music contest. Everyone played
beautifully, but King Midas, who had been asked
to judge the contest, gave first prize to the god Pan, his
favorite flute player. Apollo, the sun god, was furious. He
thought *he* should have won. After all, he was a much
better musician than Pan. In his rage, Apollo changed
King Midas's ears into the ears of a donkey!

King Midas was horrified. He locked himself in his
room, and sent at once for a barber. The barber was asked to
make a huge wig which would cover the donkey's ears, but
first he had to promise never to tell the king's secret to

anyone. The barber promised, the wig was made, and King Midas was happy once more.

But the barber longed to share the king's secret. One day, unable to keep silent any longer, he dug a deep hole in the middle of a field. He then knelt down and shouted into the earth, 'Midas, King Midas, has donkey's ears!' He felt much better. He had shared the secret, but not with another person. He had not broken his promise to the king.

Time passed. Tall reeds grew over the hole in the middle of the field. But the reeds had heard the barber's words and as they bent and rustled in the wind, they whispered, 'Midas, King Midas has donkey's ears!' Soon everyone knew the king's secret.

Even today, if you listen carefully to reeds as they bend and rustle in the wind, you may hear the story of King Midas and his donkey's ears.

A WALK IN THE MUD

IT HAD BEEN RAINING VERY HARD FOR DAYS and days. Then, one morning, the rain stopped and the sun shone brightly. A little boy and a little girl decided to go for a walk.

The rain had made the ground very muddy. Splish, splosh, splish, splosh went the children as they walked along the path. Suddenly, the little girl's feet slid from under her, and down she went, bottom first, into the slippery, gooey mud!

The little boy caught hold of the little girl's hands and tried to pull her to her feet. But as he was pulling, his feet slid from under him, and he too sat down in the same puddle of mud!

So they took hold of each other's hands and both pulled at the same time. But it was no good. They just kept falling back into the mud. Splish! went the little girl. Splosh! went the little boy. Splish! went the little girl. Splosh! went the little boy. And the more they fell, the more they laughed. And the more they laughed, the more covered in mud they became.

And do you know, they were quite unable to get up by themselves. Do you think they could still be there, in that same puddle of mud, going splish, splosh, splish, splosh, splish, splosh?

A BRIDGE IN THE SKY

LONG AGO THERE WERE TWO STARS SHINING IN the sky. One was the daughter of the King of Heaven. The other was a cowman. They met and fell in love, and the cowman went to the King of Heaven to ask if he could marry his daughter. The king agreed.

The princess and the cowman were very happy. They spent every minute together. The cowman forgot about his cows and the princess forgot to spin the fluffy clouds which keep the stars safe during the day.

This made the king very angry. He sent the cowman to live on the far side of the sky, across the Heavenly River. And he decided that the princess and the cowman should be allowed to see each other on only one day each year.

When that day came, the princess hurried to the Heavenly River but could not get across. She began to cry.

A flock of geese saw how sad she was and took pity on her. They spread their wings to make a bridge across the sky. The princess and the cowman ran towards each other.

The geese promised to make a bridge every time the princess and the cowman visited each other. And if you look up on a starry night, you might see them running towards each other across their feathered bridge.

THE THREE BILLY GOATS GRUFF

THE THREE BILLY GOATS GRUFF LIVED IN A grassy meadow on the banks of a fast-flowing stream. One day, when the grass in their meadow was almost eaten, they decided to cross to the other side of the stream where the grass looked thick and juicy.

But first they had to cross the bridge, and under this bridge lived a great, ugly Troll.

The first to cross the bridge was the youngest Billy Goat Gruff. Trip-trap, trip-trap, he went. The Troll woke up with a snarl.

'Who's that trip-trapping over my bridge?' he roared.

'It's only me, the youngest Billy Goat Gruff. I'm going over the bridge to eat the thick, juicy grass in the field on the other side.'

'Oh, no, you're not!' said the Troll. 'I'm coming to gobble you up!'

'Oh, please don't eat me,' begged the youngest Billy Goat Gruff. 'I'm much too thin and small. Why don't you wait for my big brother? He'll make a much nicer meal.'

'Oh, all right,' snarled the Troll. 'Over you go.'

Sure enough, the second Billy Goat Gruff soon came over the bridge. Trip-trap, trip-trap, he went.

'Stop!' roared the Troll. 'Who's that trip-trapping over my bridge?'

'It's me, the second Billy Goat Gruff,' came the reply. 'I'm going over the bridge to eat the green grass on the other side.'

'Oh, no, you're not!' said the Troll. 'I'm coming to gobble you up!'

'There's no point in eating me,' laughed the second Billy Goat Gruff. 'You should wait for my big brother. He's much bigger and fatter.'

'Oh, all right,' said the Troll in a grumpy voice. 'Over you go.'

Just then, along came Big Billy Goat Gruff. Trip-trap, trip-trap went his hoofs.

'Who's that trip-trapping over my bridge?' roared the great, ugly Troll.

'It's me, Big Billy Goat Gruff,' said the goat in his very loud voice.

'Well, I'm coming to gobble you up!' screamed the Troll. And he leapt up on to the bridge, rolling his greedy eyes and licking his fat lips.

But Big Billy Goat Gruff just lowered his head and rushed at the Troll. He butted him with his horns and tossed him off the bridge, over the fields and meadows and across the mountains, far, far away.

From then on, the three Billy Goats Gruff crossed the bridge every day to feed on the juicy green grass on the far side of the stream.

THE MAGIC POT

ONCE UPON A TIME, THERE WAS A LITTLE GIRL who lived with her mother in a tiny house near a small town. They were very poor and often went hungry. Sometimes they had nothing to eat at all.

One morning, while the little girl and her friends were picking blackberries in the nearby wood, they met an old woman who was carrying an empty iron pot.

'Take this pot,' said the old woman, putting the pot into the little girl's hands. 'When you are hungry, say LITTLE POT, BOIL. And when the pot has cooked enough food for you, say LITTLE POT, STOP!'

The girl was surprised by the old woman's gift, but she took the pot home. And sure enough, as soon as she said 'LITTLE POT, BOIL', the pot began to bubble and hiss and steam. Soon it was filled with the creamiest, most delicious porridge the girl and her mother had ever tasted. Just before the porridge overflowed, the little girl said, 'LITTLE POT, STOP!' And it did! It really was a magic pot. The girl and her mother would never be hungry again.

One day when the little girl and her friends were out picking mushrooms, her mother set the pot on the table and said, 'LITTLE POT, BOIL'. Once more, the pot began to bubble merrily. But as the porridge rose to the top of the pot, the girl's mother found to her horror that she couldn't remember how to make the pot stop!

'Stop, stop!' she shouted. But the pot went on bubbling. 'PLEASE stop!' she tried again. But it was no

good. The porridge began to trickle over the edge of the pot and on to the floor.

'Oh, no! Please, I don't want any more,' cried the mother. But by now the porridge was bubbling out of the front door and into the street.

It ran down the street and into the town. It flowed into houses and shops, and filled up the drains.

'What on earth is going on?' said the townspeople as they waded through the sticky mess.

'It's the pot! It won't stop!' wailed the girl's mother. Soon *everyone* was shouting at the pot to make it stop.

The little girl heard all the shouting and ran home as fast as she could. As soon as she saw the river of porridge, she realized what had happened.

'LITTLE POT, STOP!' she shouted breathlessly as soon as she entered the house. And, of course, the little pot did stop, because the girl had used the correct words!

The girl's mother promised never to use the pot again unless her daughter was at home. All the townspeople were very glad. It took simply ages to clean up the town, and they certainly didn't want to have to do that again!

THE MISSING DONKEY

ONE DAY, ABU ALI WENT TO THE MARKET AND bought five donkeys. He rode home on one of them, while the rest followed behind.

Halfway home, Abu Ali stopped. 'I must count my donkeys,' he said to himself, turning around.

'One, two, three, four. Oh, no! Where's five?'

He jumped down from his donkey. He looked behind the rocks and trees. But there was no donkey to be seen.

'I'll count them again. Perhaps I made a mistake,' he said. 'One, two, three, four, five! Oh, thank goodness,' he cried. 'He must have come back!'

So Abu Ali climbed on to his donkey and trotted on.

But soon he stopped again and turned around to count his donkeys once more. There were only four! So down came Abu Ali from his donkey. 'I will count again,' he said. And this time there were five.

Abu Ali was very puzzled. Just then he saw his friend Musa. 'I keep losing one of my donkeys, Musa,' he called. 'When I turn around to count, I have only four. But when I get down to count, I have five!'

'You silly old thing,' laughed Musa. 'You've forgotten that you're riding one of the donkeys! When you turn around, you count only the four donkeys behind you and forget to count the one you're sitting on!'

Abu Ali rode home with a red face. He did feel silly!

THE BOY WHO DIDN'T
TELL THE TRUTH

T HERE WAS ONCE A FARMER WHO LIVED IN A
village in France. One day he sent his youngest
son to look after the sheep. But no sooner had the
boy left than he was back again.

'Father! Come quickly!' he cried. 'I've just seen a hare
in the field. It was as big as a horse!'

'A hare as big as a horse?' laughed his father. 'Don't
be silly!'

'Well, perhaps it was as big as a little horse,' suggested
the boy.

'I've never seen a hare even that big, son,' said the
farmer, scratching his head.

'Well, perhaps it was as big as a calf,' said the boy.

'Oh, I don't think so,' came the reply.

'Well, perhaps it was as big as a sheep? Or maybe a
lamb?'

The farmer chuckled to himself.

'Well,' his son began again, 'perhaps it was as big as a
cat? Or a mouse? Or even a fly?'

'Oh, son,' said the farmer, shaking his head. 'A fly is
tiny. How could a hare possibly be as big as a fly? I don't
believe you saw anything at all!'

And he sent his little boy, who sometimes told the
truth and sometimes didn't, back to look after the sheep.

THE PIXIES' FLOWERS

AN OLD WOMAN CAME TO LIVE IN A BEAUTIFUL cottage near the edge of a forest. The garden was very overgrown, and the old woman worked hard to clear it of weeds. She toiled all through the hot summer and the cold winter until her back ached and her hands grew rough and sore. But at last, the garden was as pretty as a picture. The scent of hundreds of brightly colored flowers filled the air, and many butterflies and birds made their home there.

The old woman's favorite flowers were tulips, and she soon discovered that these were the pixies' favorite flowers too! Every night when the tulips were in bloom, the pixies came and sang their babies to sleep in tulip cradles. Sometimes the wind made the tulips rock gently, and as they rocked the pixie mothers danced softly, keeping time with the nodding of the flowers.

The old woman often heard the pixies singing in the moonlight, as their sweet voices floated through her open window with the scent of the flowers. But she hardly ever saw them, for as soon as the sun rose, the pixies took their babies from the tulip cradles and returned to their homes which are hidden under the ground in the places the flowers come from.

The tulips in the old woman's garden grew lovelier every year and people came from far and near to look at them. When the tulips were in full bloom, they made the garden look as if a bit of rainbow had fallen from the sky.

SHIRO, THE FAITHFUL DOG

L ONG AGO, IN JAPAN, THERE LIVED AN OLD man, an old woman, and their dog, Shiro.

The old man and woman were poor and they lived a simple life. All they wanted was enough money to buy rice for themselves and Shiro. But year by year their savings grew smaller. They worried that soon there would be no money for rice.

One day the old man and woman were working hard in their garden. Shiro ran here and there, sniffing the ground. Suddenly he started digging a hole in the earth and barking loudly.

'Be quiet, Shiro,' said the old woman.

But Shiro kept barking and digging, so the old man went to see what the dog had found. He poked a stick into the hole and felt it strike something hard. He dug a little further and uncovered a small box. When he opened the box he was amazed to see that it was full of gold coins!

'Wife, come and look at this!' he cried excitedly. 'There is enough money here to buy rice for the rest of the year. We shall not go hungry!'

Tears of joy came into the old woman's eyes as she saw the sparkling coins. 'Thank you, Shiro,' she said, bending down to stroke the dog. 'What a good and faithful friend you are.'

But a greedy neighbor heard about the old couple's good fortune and he was jealous. So he followed Shiro everywhere, hoping to find another box of treasure. He

dug holes wherever the dog sniffed, but he found nothing. Finally the neighbor flew into a rage. He chased poor Shiro and killed him.

The old couple cried when they learned that Shiro was dead, for they loved the dog dearly. Then one night the ghost of Shiro appeared to them in a dream.

'You loved and cared for me,' said Shiro's ghost, 'and now I shall care for you. Tomorrow, you must cut down the old pine tree in the garden. Mix some tiny pieces of wood from the tree into a pot of rice.' Then the ghost vanished as suddenly as it had appeared.

The next day the old man chopped down the pine tree and the old woman cooked a pot of rice. She stirred in the tiny pieces of wood and peered into the pot.

'Look!' she cried. 'Each grain of rice is turning into a gold coin! We shall have money for rice for the rest of our lives!'

The old couple smiled as they thought of Shiro. Even though he had died, their good and faithful dog had not forgotten them.

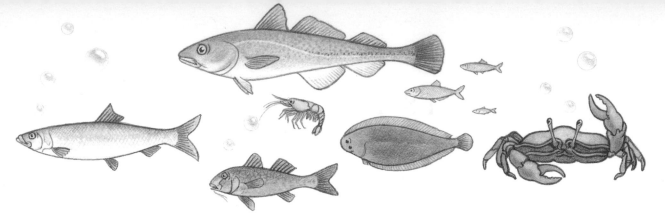

THE KING OF THE FISH

WHEN THE WORLD'S SEAS WERE YOUNG, THE fish which swam in them were very badly behaved. They swam this way and that, not watching where they were going and not caring who they bumped into. The biggest fish weren't hurt very often, but the tiniest fish were so bruised and scratched that they began to spend most of their time hiding in the seaweed.

Soon all the fish were fed up. They wanted the sea to be a pleasant, peaceful place. 'It's time we had a King,' they said. 'We need someone to look after us.'

It was decided that the King of the Fish should be the fastest swimmer, so a race was held. The cod, the herring, the sole, the mullet, the prawn and many others all lined up at the start. At a signal from the crab, they set off. At first the mullet was in front, but the herring soon caught up. The sole and the others swam furiously behind.

Suddenly a cry was heard. 'The herring has won!'

'Impossible!' shrieked the sole. 'The herring can't possibly have won! He's so ugly!' And he twisted his face into a bad-tempered scowl.

The herring, the new King of the Fish, had to tell the sole off for behaving badly. And what do you think the sole's punishment was? Yes, you're right, the sole has never lost that bad-tempered scowl!

GIFTS FROM THE STARS

ONCE UPON A TIME THERE WAS A LITTLE GIRL who was very poor and often did not have enough to eat. But she was a kind little girl and always shared whatever she had with people poorer than herself, no matter how little she had to give.

One day, when she had given her last loaf of bread to a poor old man and wrapped her ragged coat around a sick child, she found herself on the edge of a wood. She was hungry and cold, but she had no food to eat and no warm clothes to put on. Night was beginning to fall, so she decided to prepare a soft bed of leaves for herself in the shelter of the trees.

As she lay down, she smiled up at the twinkling stars. Then she looked again. Some of the stars seemed to be falling from the sky towards the wood! The little girl's eyes opened wide. As she stared, the stars landed gently among the leaves. Some of them turned into silver coins. Others changed into fine cotton dresses and warm woolen coats. The little girl laughed happily as she gathered up her gifts. She would never be cold or hungry again!

But you can be sure that this kind little girl shared her gifts with many other people.

THE GREAT BIG TURNIP

ONCE UPON A TIME IN RUSSIA, AN OLD MAN grew the biggest turnip anyone had ever seen. Every day it got bigger and bigger. It seemed to fill the whole of the old man's garden!

At last the old man decided to pull it up. He took hold of the leaves and pulled, but the turnip did not move.

The old man called to his wife to come and help. The old woman pulled the old man, and the old man pulled the turnip, but the turnip did not move.

So the old woman called to her granddaughter to come and help. The granddaughter pulled the old woman, the old woman pulled the old man, and the old man pulled the turnip. Still the turnip did not move.

The granddaughter called to her dog to come and help. The dog pulled the granddaughter, the granddaughter pulled the old woman, the old woman pulled the old man, and the old man pulled the turnip. But the great big turnip stayed firmly in the ground.

The dog called the cat to come and help. The cat pulled the dog, the dog pulled the granddaughter, the granddaughter pulled the old woman, the old woman pulled the old man, and the old man pulled the turnip. They all pulled and pulled as hard as they could, but still the turnip did not move.

Then the cat called to a mouse to come and help. The mouse pulled the cat, the cat pulled the dog, the dog pulled the granddaughter, the granddaughter pulled the old woman, the old woman pulled the old man, and the old man pulled the turnip. Together they pulled and pulled and pulled as hard as they could.

Suddenly, the great big turnip came out of the ground, and everyone fell over!

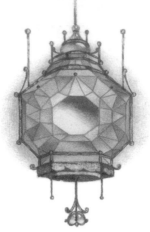

THE CRYSTAL CAVE

I N A LONELY CLIFF ON THE SHORE OF AN island bay is a cave. It has a very small opening but inside, the cave is wide and high.

A boy called Tom once dared to creep far into this cave, attracted by the faint sound of music from deep within. Holding up his candle, Tom discovered that the music seemed to be coming from a hole in the cave wall, high above his head. He put his candle on a ledge of rock and began to climb.

The hole led into another huge cave which shone like crystal. On the floor of the cave were a hundred little men and women, dancing merrily. Tom knew they were fairies, although he had never seen fairies before. On a high platform in the middle of the cave were seven fairy musicians. They played for the dancers on golden flutes and little black fiddles.

Tom was fascinated. He sat in a dark corner of the cave, nodding his head in time to the music, which grew faster and faster. The fairies danced until they were quite dizzy. One even cartwheeled and somersaulted right across the floor! Tom laughed at her antics. But as he did so, the music stopped and the dancers stood still.

'There is a stranger here,' a shrill voice called out. 'Search for him, search for him!'

'What shall we do with him when we find him?' asked one of the fairies.

'Take him to the crystal dungeon!' someone roared.

Tom looked around to see who had spoken these terrible words. There, among the fairies, stood an enormous giant with flashing green eyes. Terrified, Tom turned and ran. Behind him he could hear the thud, thud of the giant's feet and the furious screams of the fairies. Then he saw the hole. He squeezed through it and scrambled back down the cave wall. He had escaped! But he went on running, as fast as his legs would carry him, out of the cave, along the shore and all the way home!

WHY SUNBIRD IS SO SMALL

T HE SUNBIRD IS ONE OF THE TINIEST BIRDS IN Africa, so brightly colored that you might take him for a butterfly. But the sunbird was once big and strong. Here is the tale of how he became so small.

Once upon a time the sunbird was very proud. He was proud of his beautiful coat of feathers, and of his size. 'I ought to be king of all the birds,' he thought.

So he called a meeting. The birds came wheeling and dipping and soaring from the farmlands, from the river, and from the tops of the tallest trees in the forest to hear what the sunbird had to say.

'My good friends,' he began. 'I have decided that it is time we birds had a king. I have thought about this for a long time and I cannot think of anyone more suitable for the job than myself.'

To his dismay, the others did not agree.

'King, indeed,' grumbled the wrinkled old vulture. 'What nonsense! I won't have that big bag of colored feathers ordering *me* around!'

'King?' said the owl. 'Hmmm!' And he blinked three or four times very wisely. 'King? No good. He's too big.'

'There you are, sunbird,' said the swallow. 'If the owl says you are too big, then you are too big. Everyone knows how wise the owl is.'

But the sunbird did not give up. Next morning he flew deep into the forest to seek the advice of the wise man. 'Plenty of people want to grow up,' laughed the wise man, 'but this is the first time I've heard of anyone wanting to grow down!'

'Listen carefully,' he continued, handing the sunbird a piece of tree bark. 'Go home, build a bright fire and perch over it. No matter how hot you feel, do not cry out. Keep on chewing this bark while the fire burns, and you will become as small as you wish.'

The sunbird did exactly as the wise man told him. And sure enough, by the time the fire had sunk to a heap of grey ashes, he was tiny. Only his beak was as long as ever. The birds were amazed at the change. Now they had no excuse to stop the proud sunbird being king. But the owl saved the day.

'King?' he said. 'Ridiculous! *Far* too small!'

And from then the sunbird has been tiny, for even the wise man was not able to make him big again.

ONE AT A TIME

THERE WAS ONCE A VERY OLD MAN WHO HAD only one son.

'It's time you went out into the world,' said the old man to his son one day. 'You must find some work to do and earn your own way.'

So the young man set off. He traveled for many days, until at last he met a rich farmer who wanted someone to look after his sheep. The young man was amazed at how many sheep the farmer had. There were sheep as far as the eye could see, across seven valleys and eight hills! But the young man agreed to look after them.

One day, thick black clouds began to gather in the sky. The wind howled. And then came the rain. It rained and it rained, until the rivers were overflowing. The young man knew that he must gather up all the sheep and take them to safety in the hills.

But by the time the young man reached the river beside the farm, there was only one bridge left. It was a very old, narrow, wooden bridge and the sheep could go across only one at a time.

So all the sheep from the seven valleys and eight hills began to cross that shaky old bridge, one at a time. And if you knew where that old bridge was, you would find them still crossing it, one at a time.

THE THIRSTY CROW

T HERE WAS ONCE A CROW WHO WAS TERRIBLY thirsty. The weather was hot and dry and no rain had fallen for weeks. The poor crow looked everywhere for water, but all the rivers and streams had dried up. There was none to be found.

Then, just as he had given up hope of ever finding any water, the crow spotted a water jug by the door of a house. He flew down at once. But when he looked inside, there was only a tiny drop of water right at the bottom of the jug. The crow sighed deeply. His beak was much too short to reach so far down.

The crow lay down by the water jug, too tired to go any further. Suddenly, he had a good idea. He picked up a small pebble in his beak and dropped it into the jug. Then he took another pebble, and another, and dropped them into the jug too. The water floated on top of the pebbles, and the more pebbles the crow dropped in, the nearer the water got to the top of the jug. At last, the thirsty crow was able to reach just inside the jug and have a drink. He felt better at once!

The crow soared and dived and somersaulted happily. His idea had worked!

THE KING WHO WANTED TO VISIT THE MOON

A LONG TIME AGO, LONG BEFORE PEOPLE KNEW anything about airplanes and spaceships, there lived a king who wanted to visit the moon.

'He must be crazy!' whispered all the people in the kingdom. 'How can he possibly visit the moon? It's thousands of miles away, up in the sky!'

But kings are used to getting their own way and this king made up his mind that, somehow or other, he *would* visit the moon. And then he had THE IDEA.

'Of course!' he cried. 'I'll build a tower!'

All the men, women and children in the kingdom were ordered to bring to the palace gardens all the wooden boxes they had. The king's carpenters began to make the tower by piling all the boxes on top of one another. The king stood by, smiling happily.

Before long, the tower of boxes disappeared into the clouds. The king started his climb. Up and up he went. He moved slowly and carefully, for the tower of boxes was very shaky, but soon he too disappeared from view. Then the people on the ground heard a tiny, distant voice.

'I just need one more box!' came the cry.

But there were no boxes left. The king was very angry.

'Pull out a box from the bottom of the pile and send it up to me!' he shouted crossly.

Well, everyone knew that was a crazy idea, but they didn't dare disobey the king. So they did as they were told. They pulled out a box from the bottom of the pile.

You can probably guess what happened. The tower came tumbling down. And the king came spinning out of the clouds, BUMP, on to the ground.

Never again did the king talk about visiting the moon!

THE MAGPIE'S NEST

T HE DAY OF THE BIRDS' NEST-BUILDING lesson had arrived. The sparrow, the finch, the pigeon, the blackbird, the thrush, the starling, the swallow, and the wren were there, but the magpie was far away, collecting brightly colored berries and stones.

When she returned the next day, the other birds kindly offered to teach her how to build a nest.

'Thank you,' said the magpie in a very bored sort of way, 'but I'm sure I know it all already.'

The pigeon picked up a twig and laid it on a branch. The blackbird laid a second twig. The magpie yawned.

The thrush showed her how to build up the nest with more twigs. The sparrow and finch showed her how mud could make the nest strong. The swallow and other birds showed her how to line it with feathers. But the magpie kept saying how easy it all was.

Finally the birds grew tired of the magpie's rudeness and they flew off.

The magpie, of course, had no idea how to finish the nest. And she still doesn't. To this day, the only kind of nest a magpie can make is a half-lined bundle of sticks.